THE FUNNY
25 DAYS OF SILLY NORTH POLE MISCHIEF

Written By: AJ Wolski

Illustrated By: Bimantara Lestarijono

Edited By: Ben Dudley

Narrated By: AJ Wolski

For information regarding permission, write to AJ Wolski at: Question@AJWolskiBooks.com

ISBN:

      978-1-958112-14-4 (Paperback)

      978-1-958112-13-7 (Hardcover)

      978-1-958112-10-6 (ePub)

      978-1-958112-12-0 (Audiobook)

Library of Congress Control Number: 2023916472

Text copyright © 2023 by AJ Wolski

Illustrations copyright © 2023 by AJ Wolski

This edition first printing, September 2023

Contents

Written by AJ Wolski

DAY 1
BLITZEN'S RAINY RIDE

In the chilly realm of the North Pole, among the cabins and workshops covered in glittery snow, the reindeer enjoyed the last few quiet days before the busiest night of the year. But this year, something was different. The reindeer Blitzen had an unusual problem: he couldn't stop spitting!

Whenever Blitzen spoke, he sprayed. When he laughed, he unleashed a rainstorm of slobber. And when he sneezed? Well, let's just say you'd need an umbrella or possibly a change of clothes.

The other reindeer were annoyed. "Blitzen," Dancer exclaimed one day, wiping her face. "You're like a sprinkler!"

Like always, Dasher made it into a joke. "We wanted a white Christmas with snow, but we got a wet Christmas with Blitzen's spit showers!"

Blitzen felt embarrassed. "I don't know what's wrong! Ever since I munched on those Mystical Moss Chips from the Enchanted Forest, it's been spit central here!" he explained sloppily.

"Maybe you should fly in the back when we pull the sleigh," Prancer suggested. "You know, to avoid soaking us all in slobber."

The thought of Christmas Eve was now starting to make everyone nervous. The reindeer practiced their flying formations with Blitzen at the rear.

Santa, hearing about Blitzen's spitty situation, decided to take action. He called upon his team of inventive elves to create a solution. After much tinkering and testing, they presented Santa with their creation: the *Sleigh Shield 3000*. It was a see-through magical barrier that could be attached to the sleigh, protecting Santa from any unexpected spit showers or saliva storms.

On the night before Christmas, as Santa prepared for his journey, Blitzen couldn't help but worry. "What if my spitting ruins Christmas?" he asked himself. "I don't want to disappoint the children with slobber-drenched presents."

However, once they took off and were soaring through the night, the *Sleigh Shield 3000* worked wonders. Not a drop reached Santa, even when Blitzen sneezed over Spain and chuckled over Canada. The presents were delivered nice and dry, the children were happy, and Santa avoided a spit storm. Blitzen was relieved, even though his drool still wouldn't let up.

A few days later, Vixen discovered a note left by creatures from the Enchanted Forest. It read, "Dear Blitzen, we heard you tried our Mystical Moss Chips. They tend to cause some splashy side effects! But don't worry, it'll wear off soon. Merry Christmas!"

Just as the note said, Blitzen's spit slowed from a storm to a drizzle. Soon, he was back to his old self, with just an occasional drip here and there.

As the years went by, the story of Blitzen's Rainy Ride became legendary, told with lots of laughs whenever the reindeer shared tales of their adventures. Santa even kept the *Sleigh Shield 3000* in case of another stormy emergency.

And so, from the heart of the North Pole, home of countless stories of magic and miracles, came a tale of a reindeer, his spit, and the Christmas that was wetter than ever before!

DAY 2
THE SUGAR PLUM FAIRY'S FART FIASCO

PFFT

Deep in the heart of the Candy Cane Forest, beyond the Gingerbread Glade, stood the majestic Sugar Castle. It was the home of the beloved and enchanting Sugar Plum Fairy, the ruler of the Land of Sweets. She was known for her great power and her elegant leaps and spins, but one year, she almost became known for an unusual problem she had.

The annual Land of Sweets Ball was approaching. Fairies, elves, and magical creatures from all around would attend this dazzling event. But Sugar Plum had an issue: stinky gas. Every time she twirled, she tooted out a fart. Every time she swayed and dipped, a loud raspberry would rip! It was unmistakable. She had a farting problem!

It started one morning, just after she drank a magical bean smoothie made by an unfamiliar fairy from the Forest Far Far Away. "It'll give you a jolt of energy," the fairy had said with a sly smile. And it was true! She felt energetic, with the wind beneath her glittering lavender wings.

The ball was in just three days! Sugar Plum was mortified. She couldn't risk filling the castle with stinky gas and grossing out her guests so much that they couldn't enjoy their famous sweet treats!

Panicking, she rushed to see Wanda, the wisest candy witch in the land. The bell tinkled as Sugar Plum entered Wanda's little candy shop where she brewed her magical concoctions and spells.

"I've heard of your... wicked gas," Wanda chuckled, trying to hold back her laughter. "And now I've smelled it!" She burst out laughing.

"This isn't funny, Wanda! I can't be the Sugar Fart Fairy!" she exclaimed, her cheeks turning an alarming shade of bright red.

"Hmm." Wanda pondered for a moment. "This calls for a Wind-Be-Gone potion. But I'll need sparkling spring water from the top of Jellybean Mountain."

Without wasting a second, Sugar Plum fluttered out the door and up through the clouds to Jellybean Mountain, tooting a few clouds of her own as she flew. She filled a vial with the sparkling spring water and returned to Wanda, who was ready with her cauldron. The candy witch mixed the water with some glittering herbs, chanting in another language.

As she was handed the potion, Sugar Plum hesitated. "Are you sure this will work?"

Wanda winked. "Trust me! Just a sip before the ball, and you'll be the most graceful and pleasant-smelling dancer of them all."

The night of the Land of Sweets Ball arrived. The castle was shimmering with magical lights, and the air was filled with sweet melodies and happy voices. After a deep breath and a sip of the potion, Sugar Plum made her grand entrance. She twirled, bracing herself to hear a fart, but... silence! She leaped and landed with no stinky smell to be found. The potion had worked!

Throughout the night, Sugar Plum was the star of the ball, dancing with confidence. Everyone was in awe of her skillful movements and limitless grace.

However, just as the clock was about to strike midnight, she heard a series of tiny *pffts* echoing from the hall outside the ballroom. She turned around to find the source of the noise. To her surprise, it was Wanda, giggling uncontrollably with each fart she let loose.

"I was curious about that bean smoothie, so I may have tested one myself before I arrived. Then I was running late and forgot to bring the Wind-Be-Gone potion!" Wanda confessed, laughing. All the other fairies and guests joined in.

Sugar Plum couldn't help but laugh too, realizing that sometimes, it's okay to embrace the silly, windy moments in life.

From that day on, the Sugar Plum Fairy's fart fiasco became a beloved tale within the Land of Sweets – a story of grace, giggles, and the occasional gust of wind. And every year thereafter, Wanda would bring a bean smoothie and her Wind-Be-Gone potion to the ball, just in case someone needed a little help staying light on their feet!

DAY 3
JACK FROST'S WONKY WINKS

Throughout the chilly Winter Wonderlands, Jack Frost was quite the legend. Not just for his icy touch, which could turn anything to shimmering frost, but also for one strange habit. He winked. A lot.

He winked at snowflakes, at icicles, and even at the chilly winter wind. Basically, Jack winked at everything, even when the winks didn't make any sense! For example, when Mrs. Claus asked if he had seen Santa's lost hat, Jack winked. When a reindeer inquired about the icy runway, again, Jack just winked. To Jack, a wink meant *hello, goodbye, yes, no,* and everything in between.

The Winter Wonderland creatures tried to understand his winking language, but it led to all sorts of confusion.

Once, during the Snowman Craft Fair, Frosty asked Jack if he liked his new silk scarf. Jack responded with a wink, and poor Frosty spent hours pondering whether it was a compliment or not, rubbing his twigs together nervously.

At the North Pole's Got Talent contest, the craziest mishap occurred. The Ice Fairies were performing a delicate spinning dance, and, in the middle of their twirls, they saw Jack winking from the audience. Mistaking it as a sign to speed up, they spun so fast they turned into mini-tornadoes, flinging themselves from the stage in a horrendous blizzard.

One frosty evening, Jack felt something strange while he was finishing an intense winking conversation with the North Star and Little Dipper (they blinked, and he winked). Jack's winking eye felt strange and heavy. No matter how hard he tried, he couldn't open it. He rushed to the mirror and gasped. His notorious winking eye was frozen shut!

Panicking, he put on his skates and hurried over to the cottage of Elsa, the Winter Witch, known for her thawing spells. "Elsa!" he exclaimed, knocking on her door. "I think I over-winked!"

Elsa opened the door and discovered Jack pointing frantically at his eye. Being a prankster, she laughed. "Yoo hoo, Captain Jack! Arrgghhh! Looks like you're in need of a pirate eye patch, eh, matey?"

Rolling his one eye, Jack sighed. "Ha ha, Elsa. Can you fix it?"

Elsa produced her wand from her sleeve, twirled it over Jack's head, and chanted.

Slowly, warmth spread across Jack's eye, and he realized he could blink again. "Thank you, Elsa! I promise to be more careful with my winks."

The next day, during a game of Freeze Tag, Jack seemed to forget his promise. He winked at Susie Snowflake, making her think she was 'it,' which created a lot of confusion in the game.

Elsa witnessed this and gave Jack a pair of sunglasses. "Maybe these will help keep your winks in check." She giggled. "And stop others from misunderstanding your meaning."

Over time, the residents of the Winter Wonderlands learned to adapt with the help of the sunglasses. Everyone realized that a wink was just Jack's quirky way of talking, and they started enjoying the amusing mix-ups that could pop up. It helped that Jack wore his shades more often and winked a little less – though he smiled a lot more!

So, of all his snowy tales of misadventures and fun, Jack Frost's Wonky Winks became the story most told and retold in the Winter Wonderlands, bringing laughter and warmth to the coldest of nights.

DAY 4
CINDY LOU'S MUDDY MEALS

In the snow-sprinkled town of Whoville, where every home was decorated with tinsel and every heart was abuzz with holiday cheer, there was a growing concern. With the Christmas feast fast approaching, the townspeople had no clue how to handle the town's black sheep: Cindy Lou Who. As nice as she was, her unusual appetite for dirt and mudpies ruined almost every feast!

Cindy Lou, with her big, innocent eyes and her cute button nose, didn't dream of sugarplums or gingerbread men. No, instead she dreamt of the rich, earthy flavors of freshly dug dirt and mouthfuls of tasty mudpies.

Her fascination with dirt started when she was a toddler. While the other kids were making snow angels, Cindy Lou made mud angels... which she then ate. As she grew older, her taste buds developed a liking for mud pies, clay cakes, and even the occasional peppermint dirt smoothie.

When Cindy Lou was invited for dinner at Martha May Whovier's house, the host served her prized cherry pie, certain that the young girl would love it. But Cindy, with a glint in her eye, grabbed a handful of dirt from the closest indoor plant and molded it into a pie on her plate, proud of her work. "This is perfect!" she chirped, licking her lips.

Martha May, ever the polite Whovian, tried to keep a straight face but ended up excusing herself to "grab additional refreshments" (and maybe gag a little).

Invitations to dinner at the Who residence were rarely accepted since everyone was afraid there would be dirt somewhere in the food.

Her best friend Annie tried to reason with her. "Cindy, don't you want something that tastes better than... THAT?"

Cindy Lou smiled at the mud muffin in her hand and simply replied, "There's a world of tasty flavors in this earth! Annie, you are missing out!"

The townspeople were desperate to change Cindy Lou's cravings so they wouldn't be so grossed out all the time, so they hatched a plan. The Mayor declared a new holiday: the Whoville Food Truck Flavor Fiesta! A bunch of food trucks were parked along Main Street, each offering the most exotic, delicious, and mud-free treats from chefs and bakers from all corners of Whoville.

Cindy Lou was curious. Everyone watched as she wandered from truck to truck, sampling everything from cotton candy cupcakes to gingerbread ice cream. She seemed to enjoy herself, but the true test was when she reached a little food cart that had, you guessed it, piles and piles of gourmet dirt.

The residents of Whoville held their breath as Cindy Lou picked up a spoonful. But instead of eating it, she sprinkled it over a cinnamon pancake. She took a bite, and her eyes widened. "It's... incredible!"

While Cindy Lou didn't give up her love for dirt entirely, from that day on, she started combining it with other flavors. Fortunately, everyone found this much less revolting. And, to their surprise, some of her creations became Whoville's favorite treats. Her chocolate-mud truffle cake and her earthy caramel cookies were all the rage for years to come.

Sure, some people still hesitated to sit next to Cindy at dinner parties (just in case they got an extra sprinkle of dirt on their plate), but they gained an appreciation of her unique taste and the creative dishes it inspired.

Tales from Whoville are never short of wonder, and the story of Cindy Lou's love of dirt is no exception. It's a delightful reminder that sometimes, the strangest tastes can lead to the most unforgettable flavors. And, at the heart of it, Christmas is all about embracing and celebrating our differences, with a big sprinkle of love (and maybe a dash of dirt).

DAY 5
SAINT NICHOLAS'S STINKY SECRET

In a snow-covered European village, where chimneys puffed white clouds and kids skated on frozen ponds, a peculiar rumor swirled through the air, making its way into each home. The news was that Saint Nicholas, the generous and jolly man loved by all, actually had a disgusting secret.

And what was that secret? He loved the smell of stinky shoes! Yes, you read that right, and he had a soft spot for realllllly smelly and gross shoes, too.

You see, each year, kids would place their little shoes by the door, hoping they'd be filled with candies and gifts from Saint Nicholas. The story went that he didn't just leave treats in the shoes. At each house, he would take a moment to give those shoes a goooood sniff!

Young Anna, a curious girl of ten, heard the rumor in school and decided to test the theory. "I'm going to wear my shoes for a week straight without socks!" she told her friends as they played outside one day. "Let's see if Saint Nicholas really likes stinky shoes."

Her friend Calvin asked, "Are you sure? What if he leaves you coal instead of candy?"

But Anna was determined to follow her curiosity. For an entire week, she wore her shoes everywhere – running through the muddy fields, jumping into puddles, playing tag, and even sometimes while she was asleep! By the end of the week, her shoes could make even the bravest soul cringe in disgust.

Finally, it was December 5th, the night Saint Nicholas was set to visit. Anna placed her shoes by the door, with a cheeky grin on her face. She then hid behind the couch, hoping to catch the sneaky sneaker sniffer in action.

The hours passed, and Anna was about to doze off when a magical whirlwind entered the room through the window, and there he was – Saint Nicholas! He looked around, his eyes twinkling before landing on Anna's shoes. Picking one up, he inhaled deeply, and his eyes widened in surprise.

Anna held back a giggle as his face turned various shades of red and green. She watched as Saint Nicholas, after recovering, chuckled to himself and filled her shoes with the biggest candies she had ever seen. She couldn't believe it: the stinkier the shoe, the bigger the treat!

The next morning, Anna shared her findings with the village kids, sending them into fits of laughter. "So, the rumor is true! He really does like stinky shoes!" exclaimed Calvin, trying to catch his breath between laughs.

From then on, stinking up your shoes became a fun tradition for the kids in the village. They would each try to outdo each other, wearing the shoes on all sorts of messy and sweaty adventures before Saint Nick's visit. And every year, Saint Nicholas would leave behind gigantic candies.

The little-known tale of Saint Nick's Stinky Shoe Sniffing became legendary over time. So, the next time you get ready for Christmas in early December, remember this tale and get your shoes nice and smelly. You might end up with more candy than you've ever seen!

DAY 6
THE SPEWING GINGERBREAD MAN

In a cozy corner of the North Pole, where snow-capped gingerbread houses lined the streets and candy canes sprouted from the ground, there was one gingerbread man who stood out from the rest: Sean.

He had a gross and weird problem. Every time he laughed or sneezed (and sometimes even when he spoke), he'd vomit up sprinkles and frosting. At first, the elves found it hilarious. "Look! Sean is making dessert again!" they'd exclaimed, giggling. But over time, the charm wore off, especially when Sean would spew sprinkles all over the floor at holiday parties. Another time, he made sledding dangerous instead of fun by covering the hills with crunchy sprinkles the elves and other north pole residents would have to avoid.

Soon, Sean had become the talk of the North Pole. When everyone gathered in the village square, the Snowman, his carrot nose turned up in disgust, spoke first. "I once saw him spew a whole tube of red frosting! His eyes widened and his voice dropped to a suspenseful whisper. "It was like a horror movie."

Mrs. Claus shushed the Snowman but couldn't help adding her own complaint. "I heard it was green and gold stars last Tuesday." Collectively, the crowd gasped, and everyone started talking at once.

Though he didn't hear their discussion, Sean knew he was different, and it pained him to see friends scooting away or hiding behind Christmas trees whenever he approached. Feeling alone and upset, Sean decided to visit the oldest resident of the North Pole, Grandma Nutcracker. Her wise advice had helped more than one gingerbread man in the past.

"Ah, Sean," she creaked when he arrived. "Our very own sprinkle-spewer. How can I help you?"

Sean felt a bit embarrassed. "Grandma, my problem is ruining my social life. No one wants a frosting-fountain friend."

Grandma Nutcracker chuckled, and, after thinking on it a moment, she asked, "What if we turned your... unique talent into something fun?"

Sean was confused but curious. "How?"

With a gleam in her eye, Grandma Nutcracker proposed a plan.

The next day, residents of the North Pole woke up to find signs hung all around: Join us for the First Annual Sprinkle and Frosting Fest! With your host, Sean the Gingerbread Man!

The day of the festival, everyone showed up in the town square once again and couldn't believe their eyes. There was a sprinkle art corner, where kids could use Sean's sprinkles to create beautiful holiday ornaments. Another area was set up for frosting face-painting, where Sean's unexpected vomiting episodes splattered delightful designs onto the cheeks of giggling children.

But the main attraction was, the Guess the Sprinkle contest. Participants had to make Sean laugh and guess the type and color of sprinkles he'd... well, produce. With prizes up for grabs, the game was a hit with the whole town, with participants tickling him, telling jokes, or making funny faces to get the sprinkles flowing.

Sean, surrounded by joy and laughter, felt more loved and accepted than ever before. The residents of the North Pole realized that what they initially saw as a flaw was, in fact, a unique gift full of fun, creativity, and laughter. And, when Sean was less nervous about throwing up, he actually didn't do it as much – only when he really wanted!

From that year on, the Sprinkle and Frosting Fest became a cherished tradition. Sean no longer felt like an outcast. Thanks to his sweet spews, he was the star of the season.

DAY 7
SCROOGE'S GOLDEN STASH

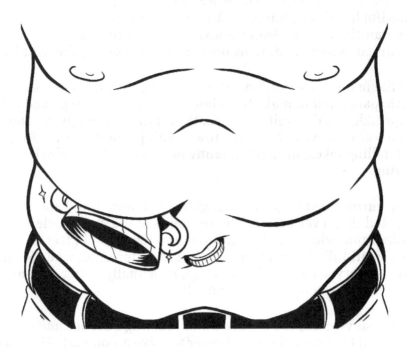

In a cozy mountain town known for its holiday cheer, Ebenezer Scrooge was known to everyone as the biggest penny pincher. But he wasn't just cheap! He was downright sneaky. There were whispers, giggles, and quite a few gasps about his new strange habit: stealing golden objects and hiding them in his belly button or the folds of his fat stomach!

At first, people couldn't believe it. "Scrooge? Popping coins in his belly button? Ha!" One by one, however, the townsfolk began to notice their golden valuables missing. JoJo, the candy shop owner, couldn't find her gold-rimmed glasses. Little Bobby discovered his golden toy soldier had vanished. Worst of all, the

Mayor almost fainted when the big gold key to the city went missing! Even though no one had seen him do it, they started to suspect the odd old miser.

One day, during the annual Christmas fair, Julio caught Scrooge red-handed. He watched Scrooge lean over a stall to admire a golden chain before snatching it and slipping it into a fold of his stomach fat! "Ewwww!" Julio shrieked, pointing at Scrooge. People started gathering around.

"What's the matter, Julio?" Bob Cratchit asked, drawn to the commotion.

"Scrooge just hid a gold chain in his belly fat!" Julio exclaimed.

"Oh, not again!" Bob frowned, not even surprised as he watched Scrooge hurry away from the gathering crowd of whispering and chuckling townspeople.

Now that everyone was sure it was really happening, it became a town game. People would lay out shiny golden objects in the open, pretending not to watch, eager to see if Scrooge would take the bait. Sure enough, Scrooge couldn't resist. As soon as he thought no one was watching, he'd quickly snatch the golden coin or trinket, slipping it into his tummy with a gross *squish*.

Kids found it hysterical. They'd burst into fits of giggles whenever Scrooge passed by, making jokes at his expense. "Oh, my precious, my precious!" they'd call after him in a silly voice. "Check his belly, maybe he's got lost pirate treasure in there!"

Things came to a head during the town's Christmas play, which featured Scrooge in a minor role. As he delivered a particularly bellowing line on stage, a golden coin fell out from under his shirt. And then another. And another. A waterfall of sweaty gold clattered across the stage!

The audience roared with laughter, thinking it was part of the show. Even Scrooge couldn't help but chuckle at the craziness of the situation, and no, this was *not* in the script.

After the play, the town's mayor approached Scrooge. "Ebenezer," he said, trying to suppress his laughter. "Why steal the gold? And why hide it in your belly?"

Scrooge, a bit embarrassed, replied, "I suppose I wanted to be rich. Not just with money, but with attention. All those years, I had felt left out of the Christmas joy. The stealing was my way of being noticed."

The mayor patted Scrooge's back. "You don't need gold or trinkets to be part of the Christmas spirit, Ebenezer. You just need to open your heart."

In the days following the play, Scrooge returned all the golden items he'd stolen, even adding a little extra as an apology. He became the most generous man in town, not just with money but also with laughter, joy, and warmth.

Remembering how much fun people had leaving gold for him to snatch, Scrooge started a new tradition. Every Christmas, the children would search for a single golden coin he had hidden in the town's giant Christmas tree. The jolly game was a reminder that, sometimes, the most valuable treasures are the ones that bring us together.

DAY 8
FROSTY'S FEATHER-BRAINED FIASCO

In Winterhaven, a small, magical town, Frosty the Snowman was a beloved figure. With his coal-black eyes, carrot nose, and magical top hat, he was instantly recognizable to everyone, and his cheery attitude made him the poster child of winter fun.

However, this year, something was off with Frosty. Every so often, right in the middle of a conversation or while playing with children, the jolly snowman would throw his head back and let out a loud "CAW! CAAAAW!"

At first, everyone thought it was a joke. "Is he doing his impression of Frosty the Snow*bird*?" asked Mrs. Butterworth, the baker, laughing from her storefront. But, as the days passed, the *CAW CAAAAW*s became more frequent. It didn't matter if Frosty was listening to carolers or judging the annual snowball fight, he would randomly stop, raise his carrot nose to the sky, and bellow "CAW! CAAAAW!"

Kids would giggle and whisper when he was around. "Why does Frosty sound like a crow?" Little Penny asked.

"Maybe he wants to fly south for the winter," joked Benny, her older brother.

The reindeer found it hilarious, occasionally following him around to catch the next *CAW CAAAAW*. "Sounds like Frosty's got the bird flu!" Rudolph said, his shiny red nose blinking in amusement.

Not everyone found it funny. Santa, who had always enjoyed his quiet chats with Frosty, now found himself jumping in surprise every time Frosty cut him off with a "CAW! CAAAAW!"

One chilly evening, a meeting was called in the Winterhaven Grand Hall. The town's most notable figures attended: Santa, Mrs. Claus, the head elf, two reindeer (Rudolph insisted on attending), and the Snow Queen.

"We love Frosty," Santa began. "But this *CAW CAAAAW* business has to stop! It's startling, yes, but it's also just not very... Christmassy."

The Snow Queen nodded in agreement. "It's disturbing the winter magic. Just yesterday, he *CAW CAAAAW*ed so loudly, one of the towers on my ice palace broke off! It was my favorite tower!"

After much discussion, they decided on a plan. The next day, Winterhaven held its very first Bird Imitation Contest. The townsfolk were encouraged to imitate their favorite birds for a chance to win a prize. After watching Frosty for so long, the whole town wanted to join in. There were chirps, tweets, hoots, and, of course, many *CAW CAAAA*Ws.

When it was Frosty's turn, he proudly stepped onto the stage. The whole town square was quiet in anticipation. Sure enough, the snowman let out the loudest "CAW! CAAAAAAAAWWWWWWW!" that Winterhaven had ever heard. The applause was thunderous.

After the contest, Santa approached Frosty. "You really have a talent for bird calls," he said. "But why the sudden interest in *CAW CAAAA*Wing?"

Frosty chuckled. "You know, Santa, when I come to life every winter, I like to try something new. This year, I found a crow's feather nearby when I woke up. I thought it might be fun to copy the crow's song. I didn't think it would cause such a commotion!"

Santa laughed, relieved that there was an explanation for his friend's behavior. "Well, Frosty, it's always good to try new things, but maybe next year, let's hope you see a bunny and then you could just try your luck at hopping."

As Christmas approached, Frosty's *CAW CAAAA*Ws became less frequent, but they never truly went away. And the townsfolk of Winterhaven came to accept and even look forward to seeing what Frosty tries out each year.

DAY 9*

BECKY THE ELF'S BOOGER BUBBLES

In Santa's magical workshop, one toymaker stood out from the rest – not because of her jingle bell necklaces or her ugly Christmas sweaters, but because of her very strong allergies! This little elf had to deal with a constant stream of disgusting boogers that would grow and grow in her nose until they erupted into massive snot bubbles. This was Becky.

With great skill, Becky could blow booger bubbles of all sizes: big, small, and even some that looked like beautiful snow globes! Others were more gross, like green slime balls or like yellow snow a dog had peed on.

One morning, a particularly yucky booger bubble floated away from her nose and landed on another elf's toy station. "Eww, Becky!" exclaimed Roger, scrunching up his nose as the bubble popped and sprayed the whole table.

"No that's... unique," said an elf named Audrey, trying to be polite (but clearly grossed out).

Becky didn't understand why they made those faces at her. She thought of her bubbles as a special talent. "Look!" she said, producing a rare clear snot bubble with a mini-reindeer prancing around inside. "It's like magic!"

Despite her enthusiasm, the disgusted reactions were pretty much the same everywhere she went. From Mrs. Claus's kitchen to Santa's sleigh garage, elves looked on in disbelief, cringing and giggling behind their hands.

Becky felt sad because she knew that her snow globe booger bubbles were beautiful. How could she make sure that all her bubbles were so beautiful and clear? She decided to go to Dr. Holly Heath, the town doctor, who told her to drink lots of water and begin taking an ultra-clear allergy pill once a day.

Now that her colorful bogeys were no more, she needed to help others see the beauty in her crystal clear bubbles. Determined to change their minds, she decided to put on a show. She made posters and sent out invites on Instagram that said *Becky's Epic Booger Bubble Bonanza! Come and see the magic!*

On the day of the show, the entire workshop was filled with nervous curiosity. Although the elves didn't want to hurt Becky's feelings, they were worried about how gross it would be. Would this be disgustingly delightful or just plain disgusting? Either way, they didn't want to miss it.

After taking her allergy pill, Becky jumped on stage, her heart started pounding and sweat began pooling in her sweater vest. She took a deep breath and started blowing the most magnificent booger bubbles anyone had ever seen. As the bubbles floated around the workshop, the elves admired the crystal clear mini-globes filled with detailed objects like snowmen, Santa's sleigh, and even one with a little Christmas tree inside!

The finale took everyone's breath away. Becky blew a gigantic bubble, and inside was a scene of Santa delivering presents. It floated above the audience, casting a magical shimmery glow on their faces.

At first, Becky was met with silence. Then the workshop erupted in applause! The elves who had once cringed now cheered in amazement, finally seeing the beauty of her creations. Audrey came forward, clapping and whooping her delight. "That was truly magical, Becky. I take back what I said!"

Roger nodded his head in agreement. "You turned something we thought was icky into something incredible!"

Santa approached Becky when she left the stage and patted her on the back. "Ho, ho, ho! It goes to show there's a bit of magic in all of us. Even in our... bogeys."

From that day on, Becky's Epic Booger Bubble Bonanza became an annual tradition. Elves from all corners of the North Pole came to see her magical art. And Becky, once the subject of giggles and whispers, became a shining example of how something seemingly odd can be utterly amazing with the help of some creativity (and maybe some allergy pills).

DAY 10
THE FUNKY FIASCO OF THE LORDS A-LEAPING

E very Christmas, the North Pole talent show was a sight to behold – polar bears juggled, gingerbread men did acrobatics, and the turtle doves did flybys that showcased their amazing aviator skills. But everyone, and I mean everyone, looked forward to the yearly performance of the Ten Lords A-Leaping. With their glittering golden outfits and high-flying leaps across the stage, they were the main attraction.

However, this year, Stephanie, the director of the talent show, noticed something different about their routine. As the Ten Lords soared through the air during rehearsals, she and the costume designer let out gasps of disgust.

31

"Is it just me, or did the Lords of Leaping bring an unexpected odor with them?" Stephanie whispered, holding her nose.

"It's like they've been dancing in a field of onions– but worse!" Rae exclaimed, trying not to gag as she prepared their costumes.

You see, their leaping was just as amazing as always. The problem was the strong, stinky smell that trailed behind them like an invisible cloud of funk. Every leap released a new wave of this nose-wrinkling stench.

Before anyone could talk to the Lords, they decided to practice outdoors one day in the town square. As they leapt, they covered the entire square in a gas that wilted flowers and made three elves faint. Even the Ice Queen, who usually kept her cool, remarked, "Their performance is... breathtaking. And not in a good way."

Santa saw how much everyone in town was bothered. Being the kind and considerate figure he is, he decided to address the issue directly. "My leaping lords," he began, walking into the town square and trying not to breathe in the smell. "Have you started using a new soap or laundry detergent?"

Lord Lenny, the lead leaper, looked confused. "We tried ordering our favorite pine-scented body wash and deodorant, but they were out of stock, so we've been practicing all-natural. Why?"

Santa exchanged a glance with Mrs. Claus, who subtly waved her hand in front of her nose. Clearing his throat, Santa continued, "Have you ever heard of something called B.O.? It stands for body odor – the stinky smell you create when you don't use soap or deodorant."

The lords had been so busy practicing, they never noticed. When they finally took a moment to sniff themselves, they were horrified. Lord Larry exclaimed, "I smell like stinky cheese mixed with gym socks! I had no idea!"

Lord Lenny got a whiff of himself and said, "And I smell like porta potty mixed with... disgusting rotten eggs!"

All the lords were shocked and worried since the North Pole talent show was less than a day away!

Determined to resolve the situation, the lords consulted the North Pole's finest elves. Lord Lenny asked the big question: "Since the store is out of stock, can you use magic to create some pine-scented body wash and deodorant for us?"

Quickly, the elves set into motion Operation De-Stink. They washed the lords' costumes in a mixture of candy cane shavings and snowflakes, followed by a fresh cookie rinse. The lords themselves needed a good wash too. Fortunately, the head elf showed up at their doorstep with his arms full of the *You So Fine Pine* body wash and deodorant they had created.

On the night of the show, as the lords prepared to make their grand entrance, the audience held its breath (partly in excitement and partly because the town square *still* stunk). Everyone was prepared for the worst. But, as the Leaping Lords leapt, they blasted a pleasant aroma of pine and fresh cookies into the air.

The crowd erupted in cheers, not just for their high-flying leaps but also for the delightful scent that now accompanied them. Even the Ice Queen smiled, announcing, "Now that's a scent-sational performance!"

And so, in the hilarious history of the North Pole, the tale of the stinky Lords of Leaping became a classic. The elves were so proud of their handiwork that they gave everyone in the North Pole some *You So Fine Pine* body wash as a Christmas gift.

DAY 11
PAPA ELF'S POOPY PASSION

D eep in the heart of the North Pole, where the Christmas spirit flows like hot cocoa, there was a resident named Papa Elf. Now, Papa wasn't just any elf. He was the oldest and wisest elf, but more than that, he was famous for having the biggest potty mouth of anyone at the North Pole – or anywhere else for that matter!

You see, since childhood Papa Elf had an unusual obsession. He could, and would, turn any conversation into one about... well, Number Twos. Yes, you guessed it: poop. Whether he was chatting about reindeer droppings, the poop-like consistency of snow, or even how certain foods resembled poo, Papa Elf always found a way to include his favorite topic.

One fine day, elf Carmen, a young chef in the making, was excitedly telling everyone about her first successful attempt at making a Mexican dinner of burritos and refried beans. But, before she could finish, Papa Elf chimed in. "Did you know that the texture of refried beans is very similar to the caca of a rare Arctic bird?"

Carmen's face turned a shade greener than her favorite moss-colored pointy hat. "Umm, thanks, Papa Elf," she said, trying not to gag. "I'll never look at my side dishes the same way again."

Another time, when Mrs. Claus presented her famous berry pie at the Great Christmas Feast, Papa Elf commented, "Those berries look just like the droppings I spotted near the penguin pond!" No one was too interested in eating the pie that year.

This happened so often that the elves even invented a game they called "Avoid the Potty Talk." To play, they would try to have a conversation with Papa Elf without him mentioning anything poop-related. No one ever won.

Santa observed the wrinkled noses and groans of the townspeople tired of Papa Elf's disgusting habit and decided to help. "Papa Elf," he began one frosty evening. "Have you ever noticed your habit of discussing poo... a lot?"

Papa Elf blinked in surprise and then chuckled. "It's natural, Santa! Everyone poops! There's even a book about it!"

Santa chuckled along with him. "True, but maybe not everyone wants to discuss it during dinner or toy-making or... well, ever."

Papa Elf looked thoughtful. "I never meant to gross anyone out. I just find it interesting and cool. There's so much to learn from it!"

Now that he realized that Papa Elf was actually interested in poo and wasn't just disturbing his fellow elves, Santa had an idea. "How about we set up a special potty talk day? One day when anyone and everyone can come to you with their poop curiosities, and you can discuss it as long as you want!"

Papa Elf's eyes lit up. "A whole day dedicated to potty talk? That sounds... crap-tastic! Count me in!"

And so, Papa Elf's Poop Day was established. Once a year, elves with strong stomachs would gather around, listen to Papa Elf's tales of droppings from different animals, learn about their consistencies, and even play trivia games like Guess That Poop! Surprisingly, many found it informative and entertaining – when in the right setting.

For the rest of the year, Papa Elf tried his best to keep his poo comments to a minimum. Though occasionally, during an especially beautiful snowfall, he'd whisper to the elf next to him, "Reminds you of the rare white snow owl's poo, doesn't it?"

Throughout the snowy kingdom, the story of Papa Elf and his poopy passion was told alongside stories of flying reindeer and magical snowmen, making him a legend. The story was a hilarious reminder that everyone has their quirks.

DAY 12
TINY TIM'S TANTALIZING TASTEBUDS

In the heart of London, the Cratchit family was well-known for their festive spirit and love for each other. Among them was Tiny Tim, a sweet, gentle boy who had a taste for something not usually found on Christmas plates: worms and beetles!

Now, London had seen its share of odd dishes in its countless restaurants, but even this was a bit much for the townsfolk. Whenever the Cratchits went to the park, kids could find Tiny Tim by following a trail of overturned rocks and logs. Eventually, they would find him sitting next to one, happily collecting his wiggly snacks. That's when the teasing would begin:

"Look at that! Tiny Tim's having lunch again!"

"I heard he had beetle soup last night!"

The rumors grew wilder and more ridiculous. One day, a story went around that Tiny Tim had a secret worm farm under his bed. Another rumor was that he seasoned his beetles with candy cane dust for extra flavor.

The kids were equally fascinated and horrified. No one wanted to sit with him during lunch at school because they were afraid of Tiny Tim chugging down a jar of live worms.

Mrs. Cratchit noticed that her son didn't have many friends and was getting worried. "Tim, sit down," she told him one day. "Let's talk about these worms and beetles. Can't you take a liking to sandwiches or fruit instead?"

Tiny Tim looked up at her with his big, innocent eyes. "But, Mom, they're so crunchy and delightful!"

His father, Bob Cratchit, had an idea. "Why don't we start a new tradition? On Christmas Eve, we'll have our usual feast, but after that, you can have a special creepy crawler treat as dessert."

Tiny Tim's eyes sparkled. "Really, Dad?"

"Really," Mr. Cratchit said, nodding. "And who knows? Maybe other people will give it a try as well."

Word got around about the Cratchit family's new tradition. Curiosity got the better of the townsfolk, and soon, a small crowd had gathered outside the Cratchit home on Christmas Eve, peeking in through the windows.

At the end of dinner, Mr. Cratchit announced, "It's time for Tim's special treat!"

Tiny Tim buzzed with excitement as he was presented with a plate of crispy beetles and a bowl of juicy, wiggling worms.

The crowd outside stood in shock until a young girl named Lucy stepped forward and knocked on the front door. "Can I... try one?" she asked timidly when Mr. Cratchit opened the door.

Tiny Tim ran to the door and handed her a beetle. She crunched on it, her face a mix of fear and curiosity. She slowly turned to the crowd and finally smiled. "It's not bad!" she exclaimed to everyone.

One by one, more children dared to sample Tiny Tim's creepy crawlers. Fortunately, Mrs. Cratchit thought this might happen and had prepared enough to go around! By the end of the night, there was laughter and delight as children (and a few brave adults) shared in the fun.

The next year, Tim's Tantalizing Treats were the most anticipated dish of the season. The once-avoided boy was now the star of Christmas Eve. While not everyone grew to love worms and beetles as much as Tiny Tim, they all learned an important lesson that you shouldn't make fun of other people for being different. When you should try to understand their viewpoints and try new things, everyone wins.

So, the next time you're invited to a unique holiday feast, remember Tiny Tim and his crunchy critters. Who knows? You might just discover a new favorite dish!

DAY 13
THE LICK-HAPPY DRUMMER BOY

Everyone who lived in the frosty, magical realm of the North Pole had their unique problems not commonly known to those residing anywhere else on Earth – especially the kids. This story is about a boy named Noah, better known as the Little Drummer Boy. Noah had a rather odd habit. He liked to lick things. All sorts of things.

Now, it's one thing to lick a candy cane or whipped cream (very common in the North Pole), but Noah licked EVERYTHING. The wooden toys in Santa's workshop? Lick! The icy North Pole signpost? Lick! The fluffy tails of the reindeer? Lick!

One time, he even licked Santa's beard! "Ho, ho, ho! That tickles!" Santa laughed, drying his fluffy whiskers, but deep down, he was quite grossed out.

Noah's curious habit got worse and worse until life in the North Pole was a moist, saliva-slipping adventure. Elves would have to wipe down their tools before using them, and Mrs. Claus took to wearing gloves whenever Noah was around, just in case he decided her hands looked "tasty." Even Santa was considering a hairnet to protect his beard.

But the real problem began when winter hit its peak. When temperatures dropped way below freezing, Noah's silly habit became a chilly challenge. His spit froze on everything he licked, making the entire town suddenly slippery. Even worse, every so often, someone would hear a muffled cry for help and find Noah with his tongue stuck to a pole, a block of ice, or a tempting candy cane.

After the third frozen tongue episode in one day, Santa called a meeting of the Council of Christmas Characters. The gathering included everyone from the Snow Queen to Jack Frost, who winked everyone a greeting.

"We have to do something," declared the Snow Queen. "At this rate, we might find him stuck to my ice palace next!"

Santa, looking desperate, asked, "Any ideas?"

Jack raised an eyebrow. "Well, I do have a solution, but it's a bit mischievous."

And so, Jack Frost's plan was set into motion. The next time Noah was about to lick the North Pole signpost, it started to wiggle. The signpost, covered in a thin layer of Jack's special snow, tickled Noah's tongue and made him pull away in surprise.

When Noah tried to lick a frozen icicle, it danced away from him, leaving him puzzled. Everywhere he tried to lick, things would either wiggle, jiggle, or downright leap out of his way.

The North Pole was alive with giggles and hearty laughs. Noah's confused expressions were the highlight of everyone's day. But the best part? His tongue stayed unstuck, and the town stayed unlicked!

Realizing the gig was up and eager to join in the laughter around him, Noah decided to give up his licking habit. But, to ensure he never felt left out or embarrassed, the North Pole introduced a new tradition: the Lickable Candy Festival. One day each year, the entire village was decked out in lickable candies of all kinds for *everyone* to enjoy. No more licking icy poles – just delicious, colorful candies. Since everyone joined in, Noah didn't feel guilty for being himself!

As the years went by, Noah's tongue always looked forward to the Lickable Candy Festival, a sweet reminder that, sometimes, it takes a village (and a mischievous frost sprite) to help someone break a licky habit.

DAY 14
JACK SKELLINGTON'S ARMPIT ANTICS

In the creepy and spooky land known as Halloween Town, there were all sorts of strange and spine-chilling characters, from werewolves to witches. But no one, absolutely no one, was as talented as Jack Skellington when it came to one specific skill: armpit noises.

Yes, Jack, the Pumpkin King of Halloween Town, had discovered a new talent. If he lifted an arm, placed his other hand in his armpit, and brought his arm down – *PFFFFT!* Hilarious farting noises (or, to some, the most revolting of sounds) would erupt.

At first, everyone in Halloween Town thought it was a hoot. "Classic Jack!" they'd laugh, slapping their knees. But as the days turned into weeks and the weeks into months, the once-amusing act became annoying. Especially when he did it everywhere he went!

Nowhere was safe from his armpit farts. He did them during town meetings, at the grocery store, and even at Dr. Finkelstein's lab, where the good doctor was often caught off guard, dropping his delicate instruments.

But the final straw was when Jack started playing his armpit during the annual Halloween-Christmas Mixer, a party where the two holidays came together to share ideas and snacks. Sally was usually supportive of Jack's jokes, but this time, she whispered in horror, "Jack! What if Santa hears?"

Unfortunately, that's exactly what happened. Just as Santa was telling a captivating tale about a mischievous elf, Jack felt the excitement of the story and let out an enormous armpit fart. The room went silent.

"Uh, it wasn't me," Jack said, looking around, but everyone knew otherwise.

Zero, Jack's ghost dog, floated away, trying to act like he belonged to someone else. Santa raised an eyebrow, and the elves exchanged awkward glances.

The citizens of Halloween Town were completely fed up. Whenever Jack approached, everyone suddenly remembered an urgent errand they had to run. Nobody wanted to risk another bad armpit episode, especially if Santa might be around.

Feeling shocked, Jack found Sally. "I don't understand," he said. "I thought it was funny."

Sally, ever the voice of reason, replied, "It's not the noise, Jack. It's the timing. There's a time and place for everything, including armpit farts."

Taking this to heart, Jack decided to channel his new talent into something productive. He started the Halloween Town School of Comedy, teaching young monsters, ghouls, and witches the art of timing in humor. The school became an instant hit!

As for the armpit noises? Jack reserved them for special comedy nights where everyone came prepared to laugh and where Santa was always the guest of honor, laughing louder than anyone else. As it turned out, even Santa couldn't resist a good armpit fart – when it was timed just right.

DAY 15
MRS. CLAUS THE CRUMBY MUNCHER

Santa Claus, with his jolly laughter and rosy cheeks, has long been the subject of many Christmas tales. But this year, new stories were being told – all about Mrs. Claus and how she couldn't stop talking with her mouth full.

Mrs. Claus was a fantastic baker. Her cookies, cakes, and pies were legendary. She loved tasting her creations often and generously. The only problem was that she also loved chatting. And lately, she had combined her two passions, munching and talking non-stop, much to everyone's dismay.

This wasn't as much of a problem around the workshop, where the elves were too busy to talk much. However, at the annual North Pole Party, Mrs. Claus arrived with a plate piled high with her gingerbread and sugar cookies, ready to share the latest gossip about the elf soccer league. Only, her words came out more like, "*Mmfph...* Elfie scored *mmfph...* two goals!" Each time she spoke, she sprayed crumbs two to three feet in every direction.

The elves exchanged wide-eyed looks. Glitter, the eldest elf, whispered to Tom, "Did you get any of that?" Tom shook his head, brushing cookie crumbs off his hat.

Santa, noticing the slightly disgusted looks, ducked under an airborne crumb and tried to change the topic. "How about those reindeer games, eh?"

But this just made Mrs. Claus start talking and munching even faster. "*Mmmph...* Rudolph had a shiny *mmmph...* nose trick!" She laughed, sending a wad of spit and gingerbread rocketing through the air.

Prancer nearly choked on his carrot. "Did she say something about Rudolph?" he asked Vixen quietly, as the two dodged crumbs.

One evening, at bedtime, Santa gathered the courage to bring it up. "Dear," he began hesitantly. "Have you noticed that you've been... well... speaking with your mouth full, lately?"

Mrs. Claus looked surprised. "Oh, I didn't notice. I just get so excited having company over and sharing my news!"

Santa spoke gently. "It's just that, sometimes, the news gets... ummm, lost in the food?"

It then dawned upon Mrs. Claus. "Oh dear! I've become a crumby muncher!"

Santa chuckled. "That's one way to put it."

Determined to fix the situation, Mrs. Claus tried various solutions. The next day, she tried silent snacking, but it lasted only minutes before she burst into a story about Frosty's new hat. She attempted a bite-talk-bite rhythm, making sure to only do one at a time. But she often forgot the order, resulting in more *mmmph*s than before.

Seeing her struggle, the elves decided to put their invention skills to good use, creating what they called the Chatty Chime. They attached it to a necklace and gave it to her to wear. Every time Mrs. Claus began to talk with food in her mouth, the chime would ring, reminding her to swallow first.

Initially, the North Pole sounded like a clock shop, with chimes going off every few minutes. But slowly, Mrs. Claus started catching herself, and the chimes rang less frequently.

Christmas Eve dinner was the real test. As everyone enjoyed a huge feast, Mrs. Claus began sharing a tale. Everyone braced for flying food when she took a bite during the story. But she paused, swallowed her food, and then continued. The hall erupted in applause!

Laughing, Mrs. Claus said, "It took some effort, but no more crumby news from me!"

So, among all the tales of flying reindeer and magical elves, the story of Mrs. Claus and her crumby munchies became a humorous chapter in the chronicles of the North Pole, teaching everyone that sometimes, it's worth waiting for the words to come (and the food to be swallowed).

DAY 16
KRAMPUS'S BURPTASTIC CHRISTMAS

BELCH & BURP

Deep in the heart of a snowy village nestled between towering mountains, children whispered tales of Krampus, the Christmas creature known for teaching naughty bad kids a lesson. However, this year, Krampus had an embarrassing problem of his own: he couldn't stop burping!

It began after he gulped down an energy drink called Frosty Fuel Fizz. The label read, *Guaranteed Jolly Jolts!* And energy and jolts he got, in the form of LOUD, echoing belches.

Krampus was worried. "I'm supposed to be menacing and frightening, not burpy and bizarre!" he exclaimed, after a particularly thunderous belch echoed through his cave.

Realizing he needed help to fix the situation, Krampus went to visit Jane the Elf, the village's best potion-maker. He tried to explain his problem, but every few words, a burp would interrupt him. "I need – *BUUURP* – your help – *BELCH*."

Jane chuckled. "Sounds like you've got a case of the Jolly Jolts! I've got just the thing." She started mixing various ingredients: moldy mistletoe, stale fruit cake, a touch of ginger, and of course, a foul-tasting secret ingredient.

"All you need is this Anti-Burp Brew," she said, handing Krampus a bubbling green potion that reeked like dead fish and rotten eggs.

Krampus eyed it suspiciously. "Are you sure this will – *BUURRRPP* – work?"

Jane nodded. "One sip and you'll be belch-free. But remember, it lasts only for 24 hours."

Grateful, Krampus took the potion and waited for Christmas Eve. As children went to bed, whispering about whether they'd been good or bad, Krampus began his rounds. He closed his eyes and held his nose as he drank the Anti-Burp Brew and headed into the village.

At first, everything went perfectly. Krampus managed to sneak around, casting his watchful eye over the kids without a single burp. He glided through the shadows like a ninja, not waking a single soul.

However, as he neared the village square, he found the leftovers from the grand feast that were still laid out after everyone went home to bed. There were pies, cakes, and... an entire table of Frosty Fuel Fizz!

Unable to resist, Krampus snuck a bottle and took a big gulp. Instantly, he let out the five loudest burps he'd ever produced: *BURP – BURRRRP – BURRRRPPPPP – BUUUUUUURRRRRPPP – BBBUUUUURRRPP.* They echoed through the village, waking nearly all the children from their slumber and setting off the town's Christmas bells!

Startled villagers came running outside, only to find a very embarrassed Krampus covering his mouth. Jimmy, a mischievous boy known for his funny jokes, pointed and laughed. "Looks like Krampus got a taste of his own medicine this year!"

Instead of feeling angry or embarrassed, Krampus chuckled. "You got me there, Jimmy," he said with a smile.

Jane the Elf appeared from the crowd, holding a tray of Frosty Fuel Fizz. "Thought you could use a bit of holiday cheer, Krampus!" she said, winking.

The entire village joined in the laughter, and, for the first time, Krampus was providing them with fun, not fear. And so, a new tradition began. Every Christmas Eve, alongside the grand feast, the villagers held a Burp-Off contest, and the champion always got an extra present.

Krampus learned that sometimes, even the scariest creatures need a little laughter in their lives. From that year on, Christmas in the village was filled with joy, laughter, and the occasional very airy Jolly Jolt!

DAY 17
THE MOUSE KING'S BELLY BANTER

Despite the countless stories told about the North Pole, there is an entire kingdom that few know about, located just beneath the floorboards: the realm of mice. Among them, there was one mouse who was always the center of attention, not necessarily for the best reasons – the chubby Mouse King.

Now, the Mouse King had always loved three things: eating cheese, eating more cheese, and admiring his plump belly. Recently, he had discovered a fourth joy – squeezing his stomach fat and making it look like a mouth. He'd pinch two sides of his round belly, making his fat move up and down like talking lips, and then he'd make silly, muffled comments: "Mmm-mmm! Cheese, please! Ha ha ha!"

While it was all in good fun, most of the mice were disgusted and confused. It didn't help that space was limited under the floorboards, making it hard to escape the belly talk.

"Did the King's belly just... talk?" Doug, the chief mouse advisor, asked, clutching his tiny spectacles in disbelief the first time he witnessed this behavior.

Jade, a teenage mouse with a flair for drama, exaggerated her disgust every time the King did it. "I think I lost my appetite for cheese... and that's really saying something!"

Yet the Mouse King seemed completely unaware of the gasps and groans. He found it hilarious when he gulped down some cheese soup, and then, squeezing his tummy, made it say, "Yum yum, that was some good soup!"

The final straw came during the Grand Christmas Cheese Ball. As mice from neighboring realms arrived, dressed in their best outfits, the Mouse King realized this was a golden opportunity to show off his new "talent." As Lady Mozzarella approached to greet him, the Mouse King's belly suddenly whispered, "Looking sharp, Lady M!"

Lady Mozzarella, ever the dignified mouse, simply raised an eyebrow and muttered, "Indeed," before quickly hurrying away with a look of disgust.

Using magic, Santa shrunk himself in size to attend the annual Christmas Cheese Ball under the floorboards. He tried a piece of cheddar and was also treated to the belly's voice. "Ho, ho, ho! Merry Cheesemas, Santa!" the belly exclaimed.

Santa just gave a polite chuckle. "Well, that's a new one." He made a mental note to discuss it with Mrs. Claus as he left.

Seeing everyone's reactions, Marcus, the Mouse King's best friend, decided to intervene. "Your Highness," he began cautiously. "Have you noticed that not everyone is... um, entertained by your... belly talks?"

The Mouse King looked surprised, "But it's hilarious! Look!" He grabbed his gut, and, once again, his belly asked for more cheese.

Marcus sighed, "It's a bit... well, cheesy. Maybe you could find another fun thing to do? Like, I don't know, belly dancing?"

The Mouse King considered this. "No talking, just dancing? Hmm..."

The very next day, the Mouse King arranged for belly dancing lessons. To everyone's relief, he was hooked! His big belly swayed and jiggled like a bowl full of jelly, but at least it wasn't trying to have a conversation.

The mice were happy. Doug noted, "It's definitely an improvement. And good exercise too!"

Jade gave a huge sigh in relief. "Thank the cheese gods, the belly has been silenced!"

Even though a belly-dancing Mouse King might not be the first thing you think of when you hear about the North Pole's stories of magic and wonder, this tale always brings a smile to everyone's face, even if it's a little cheesy.

DAY 18
COMET'S BUBBLE BLAST

In a snowy pasture near Santa's Workshop, the reindeer played games, practiced flying, and chatted with each other. There was one reindeer who now stood out from the rest: Comet. Not because he was the fastest or the strongest, but because Comet had a strange and captivating talent: he could blow massive spit bubbles.

Every time the reindeers gathered for a break, Comet would start his show. He'd gather up some spit, purse his lips, and slowly, a big, shimmering bubble would emerge and float through the cold air before popping in a tiny, wet explosion. It was fascinating and, well, a bit icky.

"I don't get it," Dasher would huff. "Why does he always do that? It's so gross!"

Prancer, ever the graceful one, nodded in agreement. "It's simply undignified. We're majestic creatures of the sky, not bubble-blowing clowns!" He winced as another bubble popped nearby.

While many of the reindeer found Comet's habit disgusting, they couldn't ignore the fact that he was becoming increasingly popular among the elves.

"Did you see the triple bubble Comet did yesterday?" an elf would ask, eyes wide in awe.

"Yeah, and that spiral one? Incredible!" another would reply.

Soon, word got around to the reindeer that even Santa liked the spitty bubbles. The whispers among the reindeer grew louder. "Why does Comet get all the attention?" Vixen grumbled. "He's just making spit bubbles!"

Cupid, the most understanding of the group, tried to calm everyone. "You know, it's just a fun talent. No need to be jealous."

But the truth was, the reindeer *were* jealous. They couldn't understand why someone as "gross" as Comet was getting all the attention.

One day, Dasher had an idea. "If bubbles can make a reindeer famous, then bubbles we shall make!" That evening, the reindeer gathered berries, squished them, and attempted to blow bubbles using berry juice. It seemed like a great plan, but all they ended up with was a sticky mess.

Having heard about their attempted bubble-making experiment, the next day, Comet approached the group. "Want some tips?" he offered with a wink.

The reindeer were surprised. They had expected Comet to brag, but instead, he was offering to share his "icky" talent.

Under Comet's guidance, the reindeer tried blowing berry bubbles again. While they couldn't produce the same size of bubbles, they did manage some small ones, leading to heaps of laughter and fun.

The lesson was clear. It wasn't about the bubbles! It was about the joy they brought. The reindeer discovered that talents can be impressive and enjoyable – even if they are also a bit disgusting.

That Christmas, the reindeer had a surprise for the children of the world. As bubbles floated down from the sky, popping as they landed, each child received something extra. Along with their gifts, they found a shimmering bubble solution as a little gift from Comet and his fellow reindeer, reminding everyone that it's our unique differences that make us special.

DAY 19
THE GRINCH'S GROSS MUNCHIES

High above Whoville, on the solitary peak of Mount Crumpit, lived the Christmas-hating Grinch. While the citizens of Whoville were well acquainted with his disgust for holiday cheer, there was another reason they'd wrinkle their noses whenever the Grinch's name was mentioned: his gross eating habits.

Yes, the Grinch was no ordinary eater. He had a knack for mixing foods that were never meant to be together. For breakfast, he'd pour orange juice over his cereal instead of milk. For lunch, he loved peanut butter and pickle sandwiches. But dinner time was the worst; he would eat ice cream with a drizzle of ketchup or spaghetti topped with whipped cream and cherries.

One day, Cindy Lou Who's curiosity led her to visit the Grinch and ask about his odd food combinations. As she reached his cave, she spotted him preparing what appeared to be a salad. But, upon closer inspection, she realized the greens were actually seaweed, and the croutons were... gummy bears.

With a mix of horror and confusion, Cindy Lou asked, "Mr. Grinch, why do you eat such a strange mix of foods?"

The Grinch looked up with a glint in his eye. "Why, little Cindy, doesn't everyone enjoy a seaweed-gummy salad? It's crunchy, chewy, and very Grinchy!"

Cindy Lou tried not to look disgusted as he took a bite. "But don't you want to try normal food, Mr. Grinch?" she asked.

The Grinch smirked. "Normal is boring. Have you ever tasted my famous mashed potato pancakes with chocolate syrup? It's delicious, and I try new flavors every day!"

News of Cindy Lou's visit and their conversation spread throughout Whoville. Soon, everyone was talking about it, and it was not helping the Grinch's popularity in town. In fact, Martha May Whovier nearly fainted upon hearing about his beloved tuna fish cookies.

The Mayor called a meeting to address what the town paper had called the "Grinch's Gross Munchies." Before the Mayor could begin the meeting, voices rang out from the crowd. "He's trying to ruin food for us!" shouted one. "Just like he tried to spoil our Christmas!" exclaimed another.

Desperate to bring some sense into the situation, Cindy Lou stood up. "Maybe we're all being a bit too judgmental. So what if he likes weird food combinations? That's his choice."

Before anyone could respond, a large shadow fell over the square. Everyone turned to see that the Grinch had come down from Mount Crumpit with a cart stacked tall with his creations.

"I heard you all were curious about my food. How about a sample?" he asked, offering a plate of jellybean-covered pizza to Martha May.

Most of Whoville backed away in horror, but brave little Cindy Lou decided to take a bite. As she chewed, her face went from thoughtful to a surprised expression of happiness. "It's... different. But not terrible."

Encouraged, a few more Whos tried the Grinch's creations. While many still found them weird, they had to admit there was a unique charm to them. They discovered the Grinch had no bad intentions in creating his flavor combinations.

Realizing they may have been too harsh, the Mayor proposed a new event, Whoville's Wild Food Festival, where everyone could showcase their strangest, most unique food pairings. It turned out that many Whos had secret unique favorites, from chocolate-dipped onions to candy cane burgers.

The festival was a hit! Whoville was buzzing with laughter, weird food, and a new appreciation for the Grinch and his unusual tastes.

The Grinch, feeling accepted in a way he never had before, exclaimed, "Who knew my kooky cravings would bring us together?"

That Christmas, the town worked together to write a unique cookbook of everyone's strange recipes, which quickly became very popular. The residents of Whoville learned that meals are like holidays: it's all about everyone working together, no matter how weird the individual ingredients might be.

DAY 20
SALLY'S SILLY-SOUNDING SHENANIGANS

In the creepy but beautiful world of Halloween Town, where every day was like October 31st, they also celebrated Christmas. Jack Skellington had once grown bored with Halloween and became obsessed with Christmas, even kidnapping Santa to take his place. His trusty gang helped him with the mission, including Oogie Boogie, his sinister burlap sack buddy, and Sally the ragdoll. But that was long ago, and Santa has since been returned.

This is a tale about Sally and her strange new habit of speaking in wildly varying voices and accents.

One day, during the town meeting, as Jack outlined plans for the upcoming Christmas, Sally raised her stitched hand and asked in a deep, rumbling voice, "JACK, HAVE YOU CONSIDERED ADDING GIGANTIC ROBOT POLAR BEARS?"

Everyone turned to look at her, their jaws dropping (even lower than usual). The Mayor, with two shocked faces on his head, whispered, "Is that... Sally?"

Before Jack could answer, Sally chimed in again, but this time, in a high-pitched squeak that sounded like she sucked the air from a balloon. "I think they'd be adorable!"

Dr. Finkelstein, rolling his eyes in their sockets, muttered, "I don't remember programming her to do that."

Throughout the meeting, Sally commented on everything with a range of accents. One moment, she sounded like a British person, the next, an Australian surfer, and even sometimes a robot. The citizens of Halloween Town were both amused and, well, a bit annoyed.

As days went by, the confusion only grew. Barrel, part of a mischievous trio of witch kids, approached Sally one day. "Hey, Sally, we were thinking of playing a prank on the werewolves tomorrow. Wanna join?"

With a cowboy twang, Sally replied, "Well, howdy partner! That sounds like a rootin' tootin' good time!"

Barrel blinked a few times, scratched his head, and slowly backed away.

After overhearing this conversation, Jack approached Sally. "Sally," he began. "Is everything alright? Your voice. It's become quite... unpredictable."

Sally, with a smirk, responded like a pirate, "Arrgggh, Jack! Life is but a stage, and we are all just scallywags! Yo ho ho!"

Jack scratched his skull in confusion. "So, you're just having fun?"

Sally nodded and responded in her normal voice. "Exactly, Jack. In a town where every day is Halloween, I thought, why not spice things up and entertain everyone?"

Jack laughed and shared this news with the rest of the townsfolk. Although they had been surprised by Sally's changing voices at first, they soon started to find humor in it once they knew that she was just having fun. They'd guess which accent she'd choose next and introduced a What Would Sally Say Day, when everyone imitates her vocal gymnastics.

Sally's silly voices became another layer to Halloween Town's charm. It was a gentle reminder that, within the spooky and scary, there was always room for a little fun and laughter – one silly voice at a time.

DAY 21
THE INSIDE-OUT ELF ON THE SHELF

In a small village on the very edge of the North Pole, where twinkling lights and sparkling snow created the most beautiful scenes, there lived a group of special elves. These weren't just any elves. They were the official Elves on the Shelves sent to children's homes during the holidays to ensure they are nice and not naughty.

Among these elves was Chippy. What is Chippy like? The nice way to say it is... well... he's different. While the other elves in his village took pride in their crisp, neatly pressed uniforms, Chippy's clothes were always inside out or backward. If that wasn't unusual enough, Chippy had a gross habit of never ever washing his clothes.

At first, the other elves thought he was making a fashion statement. "Perhaps it's the latest elf trend," whispered Brookie the Elf to Leesa, her best friend. But then days turned into weeks, and it became impossible to ignore Chippy's aroma. It was a strong mix of pine, freshly baked cookies, candy cane dust, and the unmistakable stench of B.O. permeating from his unwashed clothes.

The smell was starting to cause problems everywhere. The North Pole's reindeer, with their super-sensitive noses, would sneeze uncontrollably whenever Chippy was near. Even Santa's face would scrunch up in distaste!

Amanda, the head Elf on the Shelf approached him, holding her nose. "Why, Chippy? Why don't you wash your clothes?"

Chippy just shrugged. "It's a lot of work doing laundry. I prefer little to no work, thank you very much."

The elves called a secret meeting to discuss the "Chippy situation" – a matter that could affect the entire North Pole! "We can't have him representing us," said Brookie. "It sets a bad example for the children!"

"I've got it!" exclaimed Leesa. "What if we gift him a brand-new outfit?"

So, the elves chipped in and presented Chippy with the most dazzling elf uniform full of bright reds and shimmering greens, with golden jingle bells all over. Chippy was touched.

The next morning, the elves eagerly waited to see him in his new outfit. When he walked in, they were confused because he was wearing the new outfit... inside out, with the tags still on!

The elves stared but then broke into laughter. It was just so Chippy!

Even though he was lazy, something magical happened when Chippy was sent to children's homes. Kids would wake up and giggle at the elf's inside-out clothing. It even started a new trend with elves and kids wearing their clothes inside out, just like Chippy. The world, it seemed, loved him just the way he was.

Back at the North Pole, the elves realized they'd been too hard on Chippy. After all, Christmas wasn't about being perfect. It was about spreading joy.

DAY 22
THE NUTCRACKER BUTTCRACKER

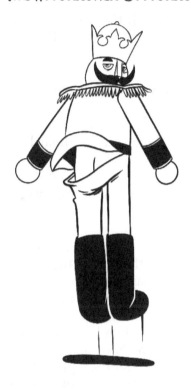

In a grand palace filled with sparkling lights and holiday cheer, all the characters from the Nutcracker Christmas ballet gathered for their annual dance show. Performers included twirling ballerinas, the Sugar Plum Fairy (who sprinkled her magic wherever she went), and, of course, the Nutcracker Prince.

However, this year, there was something a tad... different about the Nutcracker Prince. Every time he'd bow, spin, or perform a grand leap, the audience got a peek at something: his butt crack. They didn't see the whole thing (not quite a full moon), but it was hard to miss. It was as if his pants had shrunk, or he had gained A LOT of weight since last year's show.

Backstage, Clara, trying to be ever so polite, leaned in and whispered, "Mr. Prince, you might want to adjust your... umm... pants."

The Nutcracker Prince was a little full of himself and didn't understand what she meant. "Adjust what? My royal sash? Yes, it's quite grand, isn't it?"

Throughout the entire show, everyone tried to give him subtle hints.

The Mouse King asked, "Have you ever heard of a belt, Your Grace?"

The Snow Queen wrapped her frosty cape around his waist, hoping he'd get the hint.

Even the tiny gingerbread men formed a line behind him, trying to shield the spectacle from the rest of the guests. However, no matter what they did, that half-moon was still shining bright, stealing attention from his impressive dance moves.

The show's photographer was in a frenzy. In every picture of the performance that featured the Nutcracker Prince, his cheeks were the first thing you'd see! The photographer tried positioning him near tall candy canes, by a tree, and even in front of the Little Drummer Boy's biggest drum. No matter what, a cheeky sliver always managed to peek through.

Finally, the frustrated Sugar Plum Fairy had enough. With a swift sprinkle of her magical sugar, she crafted a glittery, stretchy belt and zapped it across the stage onto the Nutcracker's pants.

The Prince looked down, finally noticing his wardrobe malfunction. "Oh, my walnut shells! Why didn't anyone tell me?"

The room erupted in laughter. "We tried!" exclaimed Clara, admiring his new magical belt.

The Nutcracker Prince, though initially embarrassed, soon joined in with all the laughter. "Well, I guess I was the star AND moon of the show!"

The photos taken of the show became legendary throughout the North Pole. Each year, everyone who had been there would look at the pictures and chuckle about the Nutcracker Prince's "reveal." And the Prince? He made sure to double-check his outfit before every performance.

So, if you ever find yourself at a Christmas ballet and notice the Nutcracker Prince paying extra attention to his pants, remember this: even in the grandest of tales, a little humor and a cheeky twist can crack you up and create memorable moments.

DAY 23
THE ABOMINABLE SNOWMAN'S TICKLING TROUBLE

In the magical forests that surround the North Pole, where the tall trees glitter like diamonds and icy mountains stand tall above them, there was one resident who stood out from the rest. Bumble, a giant creature also known as the Abominable Snowman, had a unique habit that sent shivers down everyone's spines. No, he wasn't dangerous, but he was a tickle monster!

Whenever anyone saw Bumble's towering shadow approaching, they knew they were in for an encounter with some frosty fingers. With his gigantic hands, he'd grab and tickle anyone – elves, reindeer, and even Santa once! Every time he got someone,

Bumble would burst into fits of laughter so hard that snowflakes would shed from his fluffy body, dusting whoever he was tickling.

Leroy the Elf often spoke of his experience with Bumble. "I was just tying a ribbon on a gift, when out of nowhere, Bumble started tickling me and laughing! By the time he let me go, I was covered in so many snowflakes, I looked like a mini Abominable Snowman too!"

While Bumble found it hilarious, the others didn't quite feel the same. Being tickled was one thing, but getting covered in snow and feeling cold and wet for hours to come? Not so fun. So, whenever Bumble's roars of laughter echoed in the distance, everyone would hurry away, hiding behind Christmas trees, ducking under sleighs, or even diving into Santa's enormous bag of presents.

Santa noticed that the townspeople were stressed by Bumble's habit and decided to address it. He invited the lovable monster to his cottage one day. "Bumble, my dear friend," Santa began, sipping his peppermint hot cocoa. "Your tickling brings joy to your heart but leaves everyone else cold and soggy. We need to find a solution."

Bumble, feeling a wee bit guilty, nodded. He didn't want to make anyone feel uncomfortable, but tickling was just so much fun!

Mrs. Claus, always the thinker, had an idea. "What if Bumble had a tickle buddy?" She saw the confused look on Santa's face, so she explained. "Someone or something that can be tickled without feeling cold!"

Suddenly, Santa remembered a very popular toy that he had made in the past. That evening, with the help of the elves, a giant Tickle Me Elmo was created. It was a Bumble-sized version of the cute cuddly puppet, and it was dressed in a bright red snowsuit to prevent it from getting soaked!

The next day, Bumble was presented with his new tickle buddy. Cautiously, he reached out and gave Elmo a tickle. Much to his surprise, Elmo came to life erupting into giggles and wiggled in delight. The Abominable Snowman laughed heartily, shedding snowflakes everywhere, but Elmo's fur remained dry.

It was a win-win! Bumble got to continue doing what made him happy, and the North Pole residents no longer had to deal with tickle attacks or soggy clothes.

From then on, any visitor to the North Pole would see a very peculiar sight. Amongst the hustle and bustle of Christmas preparations, there'd be Bumble tickling Elmo, both of them covered head-to-toe in snow and laughing like there was no tomorrow. And everyone else? They'd be chuckling from a safe, dry distance, grateful that the enormous Tickle Me Elmo had saved their holiday season.

DAY 24
GASSY SANTA SYNDROME

All throughout the magical land of the North Pole, from the forests and mountains to the town and its workshops, everyone knew of Santa's jolly adventures. Every Christmas, he'd fly his sleigh, led by his magical reindeer team, delivering gifts to children worldwide. However, there was one secret that Santa didn't share with the residents of the North Pole. To this day, not many people know this stomach-twisting tale. You see, Santa Claus recently became lactose intolerant.

What does that mean? Well, Santa's tummy gets upset and gassy anytime he has dairy products like cheese, butter, ice cream, or milk. It started innocently enough. Children around the world, hoping to win some brownie points, would leave milk and cookies for Santa. They pictured him taking a hearty bite and a long gulp, feeling refreshed and energized for the rest of his journey.

In reality, each time he downed a glass of milk, Santa's face would turn a sickly green color. His belly, famous for shaking like a bowl full of jelly, would instead rumble as a storm of stinky gas brewed inside it.

Santa didn't tell anyone, but Rudolph could tell what was bothering him. "Why don't you just avoid the milk, Santa?" he asked after a particularly loud tummy grumble.

Santa sighed. "I don't want to disappoint the children. They leave it for me with so much love and hope. But, oh, how I wish they would just leave water or even some almond or soy milk!"

Santa's biggest fear was that he would begin unintentionally leaving behind "stink bombs." He didn't want homes to fill up with his smelly gas after each visit. He couldn't stop picturing their horrified expressions when the kids came downstairs the next morning.

Word got around in the North Pole, and Santa overheard the elves whispering about "Gassy Santa Syndrome." Meanwhile, Dasher, Dancer, and the rest of the team developed a strategy, hanging pine tree air fresheners on their antlers to withstand Santa's stink whenever he was near.

One day, not long before Christmas, Mrs. Claus had an idea. "What if we send a little note to every child, suggesting they leave out a different kind of treat?" Santa thought about this and agreed.

The elves worked tirelessly, sending out the message to children and parents everywhere. That year, when Santa began his worldwide expedition, he noticed a delightful change. In place of regular milk, he found glasses of water, almond, soy, and even rice milk! Everything was as delicious as ever, even without any dairy.

With each house he visited, Santa's heart grew full and his tummy stayed calm. It meant a lot to him that the children cared so much. On top of that, the sleigh rides were more pleasant for the reindeer (and for any birds flying behind the sleigh).

From that Christmas on, children everywhere remembered Santa's special milk preference. Homes would not wake up to a mysterious "holiday aroma," and Santa could enjoy his treats without any tummy troubles or "stink bombs."

The tale of the lactose-intolerant Santa became a legendary story shared everywhere – not just in the North Pole.

DAY 25
CHRISTMAS CHAOS AT THE NORTH POLE

The North Pole was alive with excitement. This year, Santa had invited all the Christmas characters for a grand holiday bash. As you would expect, when you get such a unique group together, you're in store for a fun and hilarious celebration.

Frosty the Snowman arrived first, *CAW CAAAW*ing like a bird every few minutes, practicing for the Christmas carols he would be belting out later that evening.

Cindy Lou Who made her entrance next, carrying a tray of mud pies and her pockets overflowing with her famed chocolate dirt. "Special dessert for tonight," she said proudly, sneaking a bite.

The reindeer were having a field day from the moment they arrived. Comet pranced around the hall, blowing non-stop spit bubbles. Dasher watched with glee, thankful that he wasn't located behind Comet in the sleigh lineup. But, one reindeer wasn't having fun. "I can't believe he's more famous than me!" grumbled Rudolph.

The Gingerbread Man, looking slightly queasy the whole time, handed out sprinkles and frosting-filled treats. Everyone complimented the beauty of his creations. But no one was too keen to take one since they knew he had vomited them up earlier – everyone, that is, except Tiny Tim. He eagerly snatched a handful of frosting, saying, "It'll go great with my worms!"

Mrs. Claus, chattering away after swallowing her mouthful of cookies, introduced everyone to the newest member of their North Pole family, Elf on the Shelf. He spent most of the evening explaining why his clothes were inside out and why there was an unmistakable aroma surrounding him.

As the host, Santa had to keep everything on track, so he started the gift exchange. Bumble, the Abominable Snowman, proclaimed that he had a gift for everyone: tickles! The entire hall echoed with laughter as he darted around tickling, leaving a path of mini-snowstorms wherever he ran.

While everyone was distracted by tickles, Ebenezer Scrooge was seen sneaking around, stashing golden items in his belly fat. He got a few but hit a snag when he tried to snatch the Nutcracker Prince's golden crown. When he jumped and lifted it off of the prince's head, on his way down, he found himself looking at a full moon, thanks to the Prince's unfortunate wardrobe malfunction.

Before Scrooge could get too embarrassed, the Little Drummer Boy began playing a tune. The song trailed off, though, because he couldn't resist licking his drumsticks instead of using them.

Santa realized that the party was already off the rails, so he told the story of his lactose intolerance, which became the talk of the evening. He explained that he had something he called "Gassy Santa Syndrome," but that his switch to almond milk saved Christmas.

The party hit its peak when Sally dramatically told the Christmas Story. She'd swap from a deep voice to an unimaginably high pitch, then shift to a perfect Spanish accent, followed by Irish, making it impossible for anyone to follow the story... but she was entertaining to watch.

As the night wound down and everyone settled around the fireplace, Jack Skellington took a deep breath (as deep as a skeleton could manage) and began an arm fart performance of "Jingle Bells," with Frosty *CAW CAAAAW*ing in the background. It was the perfect end to a long, chaotic day.

And, as everyone left with their bellies full (of laughter and food) and their hearts warmer than the coziest blanket, they all agreed on one thing: the North Pole's Christmas bash was the strangest and coolest party of the year!

Merry Christmas to all, and to all a goodnight!

Your Free Gift

As a way of saying thanks for your purchase, I'm offering a **Bonus Pack of Free Goodies!**

- **The FREE Audiobook** of The Funny Advent Calendar: 25 Days of Silly North Pole Mischief
- A Christmas Activity book for kids available for download and print
- Coloring pages of all the characters!

To get instant access use link : https://bit.ly/466EDCv

(If under the age of 18 please ask a grown-up to help you)

Inside the audiobook, you will discover:

- An unforgettable gift for kids aged six and up who like to giggle and enjoy goofy stories.

- This humorous tale is ideal for reluctant readers who may want to listen and read the book with the narrator.

- It motivates children to be mindful about eating responsibly.

About the Authors

AJ is a combination of a daughter (Audrey) and mother (Jane) writing team. They live in Henderson, Nevada in the United States. Jane has two children and two grandchildren who inspired her during their childhood to become a childrens' author. Audrey is the supporting daughter who helps her mother make that dream turn into a reality.

Please Write a Review

Authors LOVE hearing from their readers!

Please let AJ Wolski know what you thought about The Funny Advent Calendar: 25 Days of Silly North Pole Mischief by leaving a review. If under the age of 18 please ask a grown-up to help you.

Both Audrey and Jane aka "AJ" read every review and would love to get your honest feedback.

Leaving a review helps more parents and children find The Funny Advent Calendar: 25 Days of Silly North Pole Mischief and enjoy the silliness & have fun themselves!

Use the link https://bit.ly/3sI867q or scan the QR code below;

Other Works

If you enjoyed The Funny Advent Calendar: 25 Days of Silly North Pole Mischief please check out other books in various age ranges

Also by AJ Wolski:

- Spots, Dots & Chickenpox (Ages 3-8)
- Monster Crap (Ages 8-12)
- The Funny Advent Calendar: The Funny Advent Calendar: 25 Days of Silly North Pole Mischief (Ages 8-12)

Other Works

Spots, Dots & Chickenpox

This playful children's book uses fun rhymes, humorous animals, and human characters to highlight that our unique traits make us special.

Join a little ducky named **Lucky** on his exciting first day at school, as he embarks on a journey of self-discovery. Lucky's unusual looks catch his teacher's and classmates' attention, leaving everyone wondering if he has spots, dots, or chickenpox. Not sure about it himself, Lucky embarks on a quest for answers.

The Funny Advent Calendar: 25 Days of Silly North Pole Mischief

With this holiday collection of short stories, young readers and parents alike will eagerly look forward to uncovering a new, hilarious tale as they count down the days to Christmas!

In the shimmering, snow-covered expanse of the North Pole, where magic blends seamlessly with the chilled winter air, there exists a series of tales so amusingly bizarre they have been kept a secret...until now! Get the gross & hilarious behind-the-scenes stories of everyone's favorite Christmas characters which were never heard before!

Monster Crap

Beware of this hysterical and stinky adventure in *Monster Crap!* In the silly little town where pumpkins glow, and Halloween parties come alive, a wild gathering of teenage monsters is in full swing. A full moon shines bright on this Halloween night as the monsters feast on too many treats.

Made in United States
Troutdale, OR
11/17/2023